EVENING LAND
aftonland

EVENING LAND
aftonland

by Pär Lagerkvist

Translated by
W. H. AUDEN and Leif Sjöberg

With an Introduction by Leif Sjöberg
State University of New York, Stony Brook

Wayne State University Press   Detroit, 1975

Library of Congress Cataloging in Publication Data
Lagerkvist, Pär Fabian, 1891–1974.
    Evening land = Aftonland.

    English and Swedish.
    1. Auden, Wystan Hugh, 1907–1973. II. Sjöberg, Leif.
III. Title.
PT9875.L2A713   839.7'1'72   75-16172
ISBN 0-8143-1542-9

Acknowledgments

    Acknowledgment is made to holders of copyright for per-
mission to reprint previously published translations by W. H.
Auden and Leif Sjöberg of poems from Aftonland.
    "My friend," "You who existed," "The god," "It is not
god," and "If you," Michigan Quarterly Review 13, 2(Spring
1974): 138–39. Copyright © University of Michigan, 1974.
    "It is in the evening," "I am the one who goes on," "Throw
open your house to me," "Only that which smolders," "Let
my shadow disappear into yours," "Hold me in your unknown
hand," "May my heart's disquiet never vanish," and "From the
surface of my being," PRISM international 12, 1(Summer 1972):
136–38.
    "Like the clouds" and "I should like to be sombody else,"
Times Literary Supplement (TLS), No. 3,654(March 10, 1972):
273.
    "The Morning of Creation," Denver Quarterly 8, 1(Spring
1973):44–46. Copyright #B851559.
    "With Old Eyes," Mundus Artium 6, 1(1973):14–19.
    "In the Silent River," Shenandoah 23, 4(1972):76. Copy-
right © 1972 by Shenandoah: The Washington and Lee University Review.
    "Everywhere," Western Humanities Review 26, 4(Autumn
1972):350. Copyright © 1972 by Western Humanities Review.
    Acknowledgment is also made to holders of copyright for
permission to reprint previously published translations by W. H.
Auden and Leif Sjöberg of poems by the following writers:
    Werner Aspenström, "Further I Haven't Gotten," Antaeus,
Issue 15(Fall 1974): 119–23.
    Harry Martinson, "The Truths of Silence," Sewanee Review
82, 4(Fall 1974):683–84. Copyright © 1974 by the University
of the South.
    Artur Lundkvist, "A Love of Wood," STAND 15, 4(1974):
28.

This translation is dedicated to the poet and translator William Jay Smith.

contents

*See Prefatory Note.

II

III

IV

V

prefatory note
on the translation

It was agreed that I should provide Mr. Auden with as literal translations of the poems as possible, indicating alternative meanings of words, e.g., of a fairly frequent word in Lagerkvist's text, like *himmel,* which can mean (as in German) "sky," "firmament," but also "heaven(s)." After reading and discussing the poem, Mr. Auden wrote his version of it. Later, he occasionally made revisions in the manuscript in his own hand. Sometimes he made three or four versions of the same poem, if he cared for it enough. Some of Auden's translations of these poems were done at 77 St. Mark's Place (East Village), New York; a couple, I believe, at Christ Church College, Oxford, and several of them at Auden-Kallman's country home at Kirchstetten, an hour's journey outside of Vienna, Austria.

It was only after several of the translated poems had been accepted by or appeared in *The Times Literary Supplement, Shenandoah, Western Humanities Review, Denver Quarterly, Mundus Artium, PRISM international,* and *Michigan Quarterly,* that I suggested to Mr. Auden that he translate the entire book *Aftonland,* and he agreed. The poems published in these journals constitute the longer, more substantial poems, and comprise by far the major portion of the poems here presented. *Aftonland* consists of sixty-two poems, of which fifty-one are here presented as Auden's work. About five of these poems, marked "R", he wanted to revise. The remaining eleven poems appear in my literal translation in the appendix.

Mr. Auden noted that Lagerkvist, especially in earlier texts (i.e., other than *Aftonland*) used "God" while in *Afton-*

land he used "god." Auden himself said he preferred capitalization of the word, in accordance with English spelling custom, but realized that Lagerkvist had his reasons for using "god."

When I saw Mr. Auden late in August 1973, at Kirchstetten, he agreed to go over the translations during a planned visit to the United States in late January 1974. But this, of course, never came to pass. And Lagerkvist never saw his first and only book of poems translated into English—he had himself entered the evening land.

Leif Sjöberg
Stony Brook and New York,
October 31, 1974

a thumbnail sketch of swedish poetry

Sweden is rightly proud of her poetry, which took its first artistic expression in anonymously-created medieval ballads. These works underwent a revival as "folk-songs," when they were collected and published in the nineteenth century. There are numerous examples of more individual poetic efforts in Sweden. The first major ones were made by the adventurer Lars Wivallius (1605–1669), who wrote of his love of liberty, and Georg Stiernhielm (1598–1672), "the father of Swedish poetry," who employed Latin and Greek poetic forms when attempting to teach the muses "to write and perform in Swedish." His contemporary, Lasse Lucidor (1638–1674) wrote wedding and funeral poems, typical of his time, as well as drinking-songs and religious poems of considerable beauty and individuality.

As so often in Swedish poetry, *nature* is a favorite subject. This applies to poets as dissimilar as Johan Runius (1679–1713), the Finnish-Swedish Jacob Frese (ca. 1690–1729), and Hedvig Charlotta Nordenflycht (1718–1763), and Olof von Dalin (1708–1763). The first pastoral poem, *Atis and Camilla* (1761), was written by the Finnish-Sweden nobleman Gustaf Philip Creutz (1731–1785).

The genius of Swedish eighteenth century poetry was Carl Michael Bellman (1740–1795), a habitual bohemian who managed to get support from King Gustavus III, the founder of the Swedish Academy (1786). Bellman, who adapted popular tunes of the day to suit his poems, liked to perform his own songs. Combining classical mythology with vivid, realistic descriptions of life in Stockholm's streets and taverns, he created a truly remarkable set of characters.

13

Among them were Fredman, Mowitz, Mollberg, and Ulla Winblad, who danced and reveled and delighted in excursions to places of natural beauty in and around the capital.

* * *

After the enlightened French-classical poetry of Johan Henrik Kellgren (1754–1795), Carl Gustav af Leopold (1756–1829), and Anna Maria Lenngren (1754–1817), came the golden age of Swedish poetry—the first decades of the nineteenth century. During that period Bishop Johan Olof Wallin (1779–1839) wrote his numerous beloved hymns and "The Angel of Death." And Bishop Esaias Tegnér (1782–1846) penned the romantic cycle based on an Old Icelandic saga, in which he idealized and humanized the old Vikings. The American poet Henry Wadsworth Longfellow visited Scandinavia, attempted unsuccessfully to meet Tegnér, and even translated several cantos from the *Frithiofs Saga,* and *The Children of the Lord's Supper.* Longfellow also wrote about the *Frithiofs Saga* in *the North American Review* (1837), "the first truly *notable* review in America of a Scandinavian achievement," states A. B. Benson, who lists no fewer than fourteen complete English translations of the *Frithiofs Saga* (*American Scandinavian Studies,* ASF, New York, 1952). Rasmus B. Anderson reprinted George Stephens' translation of the *Frithiofs Saga* in *Viking Tales of the North* (1877), and in Britain Mary Howitt included two important cantos in *The Literature and Romance of Northern Europe* (1852).

Other major figures of the period were the Romantics Per Daniel Amadeus Atterbom (1790–1855), creator of the poetic fairy plays *The Island of Bliss* and *Blue Bird,* and Erik Johan Stagnelius (1793–1823) noted for his special mixture of religious and erotic themes.

The great lyric realist and patriot Johan Ludvig Runeberg (1804–1877), a Finland Swede, wrote *Tales of Ensign Steel,* in which soldiers of all ranks defend Finland against the Russian attacks of 1808/09. Runeberg also produced simple, intimate *Idyls and Epigrams,* inspired by Serbian folksongs. Karl Jonas Love Almqvist (1793–1866) influenced later generations of Swedish poets through his *Songes* (Dreams), with their detached, religious-mystical tone. Almqvist, who spent the years 1854–64 in Philadelphia, Pa., in voluntary exile, has been apostrophized in the poem *Professor Gustawi,* by Gunnar Ekelöf (1907–1968).

Runeberg's simple style became the admired pattern for the "Signature coterie" of the 1860s and '70s. The group's most prominent representative was Count Carl Snoilsky (1841–1903), whose later poetry reflected a certain degree of social consciousness. The same applies to the works of Viktor Rydberg (1828–1895), whose paragons were Tegnér, Stagnelius, Goethe, Nicolaus Lenau and the American Edgar Allan Poe. Rydberg's *Prometheus and Ahasuerus* confronts the idealist and the materialist. *The New Song of Grotte* draws a fantastic picture of man's suffering under an industrialism that leads to affluence of the few and impoverishment of the masses. Rydberg saw no hope for industrial society and had no faith in Marxist solutions. Rydberg's poetry dealt with man's major concerns, and yet he managed to present them in a simple, unadorned style.

Although there are occasional echoes from Rydberg in Lagerkvist, even in *Aftonland,* it is reasonable to assume that August Strindberg (1849–1912) left a deeper imprint, especially through his far-reaching symbols of life and death (as seen in *A Dream Play*). In the 1890s Swedish poetry experienced a second golden age with Gustaf Fröding (1860–1911), Verner von Heidenstam (1859–1940), Erik Axel Karlfeldt (1864–1931) and Oscar Levertin (1862–1906). These men reacted against the oppressive restrictions imposed upon poetry by Naturalism. Instead they wanted song, imagination, dream, and divination to reign once again. As a result their works exude a lyrical richness as well as some idle chaff (seen especially in Karlfeldt). A reaction against lyrical oratory came with Bo Bergman (1869–1967), who brought about a healthy reduction in the claims of poetry, returning it to a smaller scale and simpler tone.

Together with the Finnish-Swedish poet Edith Södergran (1892–1923) Pär Lagerkvist (1891–1974) is credited with having introduced "modernism" onto the Swedish lyric scene. Lagerkvist's *Ångest* (Anguish), and Södergran's *Dikter* (Poems), both published in 1916, brought a new intensity, freedom and abruptness to poetry. They also—in a more immediate fashion—reflected specific personal feeling. Both poets apparently arrived at their free, personal style independently. While Södergran was familiar with Vladimir Mayakowsky's work, Lagerkvist had been introduced to modern art in Paris by the American Gertrude Stein, among others.

Lagerkvist's new style (using free, unrhymed verse as well as traditional patterns) received more impulses from modern art—cubism, expressionism, naivism—than from literature, and was fully developed with *Den lyckliges väg* (The Way of the Happy One, 1921). However, it was refined by the poet over and over again in subsequent collections. In a provocative critical essay, *Ordkonst och bildkonst* (Word Art and Pictorial Art, 1913), Lagerkvist stated that his aim was to reach beyond the boundaries of an individual's nature and to soar to "simple thoughts, uncomplicated feelings when confronted with life's eternal powers." His essay cited religious documents, the Bible, Rig Veda, Avesta, Koran, Icelandic sagas and poetry, folksongs, Kalevala, etc., as worthy stylistic models. What makes Lagerkvist's style special is its simplicity, seriousness, and universality. In this Lagerkvist is unique. Such a claim does not necessarily imply that he "equaled" or "surpassed" poetic geniuses of a younger generation as dissimilar as Gunnar Ekelöf (1907–1968), Harry Martinson (b. 1904) and Artur Lundkvist (b. 1906).

Among the many Swedish poets who have broken the language barrier and have reached Continental Europe, intact, are Erik Lindegren (1910–1968), Hjalmar Gullberg (1898–1961), Johannes Edfelt (b. 1904), Karl Vennberg (b. 1910), and Werner Aspenström (b. 1918). Among the many excellent young Swedish poets who have been adequately translated into English are Tomas Tranströmer (b. 1931), Östen Sjöstrand (b. 1925), Lars Gustafsson (b. 1936) and Göran Sonnevi (b. 1931).

In this catalogue of Swedish poets there is a notable lack of quotations. The reason is that by and large the poets' representative works (and portions thereof) for all practical purposes are available only in Swedish anthologies. However, students who frequent university libraries might find copies of C. W. Stork's *Anthology of Swedish Lyrics from 1750 to 1925* (New York: American-Scandinavian Foundation, 1930, out of print), Martin S. Allwood's *20th Century Scandinavian Poetry* (Mullsjö, Sweden: Marston Hill, 1950, sold out), and C. D. Locock's *A Selection from Modern Swedish Poetry* (New York: Macmillan, 1930, out of print). *Eight Swedish Poets* (Ekelöf, Forssell, Gullberg, Håkanson, Lagerkvist, Lindegren, Martinson, and Södergran), translated and edited by Frederic Fleisher (Staffanstorp, Sweden: Bo Cavefors, [1963], 1969, still available), and the Sweden Number of the *Literary Review* (guest editor: Richard B. Vowles, vol. 9, no. 2, 1965–66) should be consulted. The *Literary Review* presents translations of Bo Setterlind (b. 1923), Folke Isaksson (b. 1927), Sandro Key-Åberg (b. 1922), Lars Bäckström (b. 1925), Göran Palm (b. 1931), Göran Printz-Påhlson (b. 1931), Bengt Emil Johnson (b. 1936), Jarl Hammarberg (b. 1941), and others.

Major efforts to promote individual Swedish poets have been made by such Anglo-American poets as W. H. Auden, Robert Bly, Muriel Rukeyser, Eric Sellin, May Swenson, and Robin Fulton, among others. *Books Abroad* (an international literary quarterly, edited by Ivar Ivask) has published George C. Schoolfield's essays on modern Swedish poetry; it covers current Swedish poetry in its reviews section. Mention should also be made of *Scandinavian Studies* (editor, Harald Naess) and *Scandinavica* (editor, James McFarlane).

Ideally, there should follow an anthology of modern Swedish poetry (as was indeed planned with Auden and Bly) to indicate the enormous range of variety. Instead, a few Swedish poems, translated with W. H. Auden at about the same time as *Evening Land,* must suffice. The selection from Karl Vennberg is published here for the first time.

FURTHER I HAVEN'T GOTTEN

Now I see him again,
the bird of the boundary,
partly in the light,
partly in the shade,
hear the divided cry
from a bird divided in two,
one black wing,
one white wing,
flying by accident
beside each other.
He who seeks a meaning
finds two.
Further I haven't gotten,
Though Spring has passed
and Summer flown away.

Werner Aspenström

A LOVE OF WOOD

calls for the sharpest steel, says the carpenter.
How wonderfully alive is Wood
under a shining steel-sharp axe!

How gentle the cuts through its rings
formed after the spring floods!
Inside Wood there ticks a clock
or perhaps a heart.
Wood is Time,
Stratified like waves on a shore.
Wood contains more compressed Time
than Man,
that is why it is harder, more lasting.
Wood has a fragrance lovelier than the skin of a woman.
It sweats small fruits, small golden grapes.
It shows its sex in every branch,
male and female in one, both joined together,
and doubly hard under the axe.
Who can enter into Wood and survive?
But who does not wish that he could?
The dead are laid to rest in Wood like the unborn.
(Oh, to rest there in deepest sleep
like a cigar in a fragrant box!)
Beauty must be won from Wood,
lasting life also.
It does not die like Man, suddenly
a stinking corpse.
No, Wood is alive in death
more firmly and freshly than any flesh.
With tender hands
and the sharpest tools,
I shall finally penetrate Wood,
feel Wood in my mouth and throat,
feel Wood embrace me,
firmly, securely, for ever.

Artur Lundkvist

THE TRUTHS OF SILENCE

Privately and in silence,
either they are there
or they are not.
You cannot see them:
if you could it would be easy.
They are significant
simply because they do not depend on reports and contra-
    dictions.
They are based on the truth which you have in yourself,
and the honesty with which you experience your silence.
In the long run it is they who are decisive in all small rooms,
in the infinite number of small rooms in every land.

Harry Martinson

YOUR TRUE TEA CONNOISSEUR

Your true tea-connoisseur
Makes his tea this way.
Your true tea-connoisseur
connoisseur of God, connoisseur of Man,
washes souls thoroughly
in boiling water.

Governments, Party Big-Wigs, Employers!
don't underestimate the advantage
enjoyed by souls who have been washed
in boiling water.
Your true tea-connoisseur
conscientiously knocks off the ashes
of his cigarette into the ash-tray.

Faith is good,
even when it is absurd,
but, if you wish to get into Academies,
let it stand and brew
for three to five minutes.

Too strong a faith
should be diluted with water:
sober faith is the best soft-drink
and the cheapest.

Karl Vennberg

introduction

Pär Lagerkvist (1891–1974) was not one who relished being interviewed by literary scholars or anyone else. Some years before an American, Professor Robert D. Spector, wrote the first and only published full-length study of Pär Lagerkvist in English (Twayne, 1973), he sent a letter to Lagerkvist, asking for an interview. Spector promptly received a reply in which Lagerkvist politely stated that he never granted interviews, especially not to those engaged in studies of his work.

A foreign correspondent residing on *Lidingö,* the very island just outside Stockholm where Lagerkvist also made his home, once came rather close to an interview with the secretive writer. On a sunny winter's day my friend spotted Lagerkvist on skis and seized the opportunity to attract his attention by fiddling energetically with his ski fastenings and finally by falling in the snow. The short but sturdy Lagerkvist promptly headed towards the man in distress and asked if he could help. When told that everything was all right, Lagerkvist slowly turned his skis to leave. After a long look Lagerkvist asked, "How do you make a living?" My newspaper friend said, truthfully, "I am a writer of sorts." Lagerkvist answered, quietly, "So am I. Good-bye." Then he dug in his ski poles and glided away.

In December 1940, when Pär Lagerkvist was to give an address, a summation of the achievement of his predecessor in the Swedish Academy, it turned out to be his first public speech. Lagerkvist was then 49 years old and had published more than 25 books. When he received the Nobel Prize for literature, at the subsequent obligatory press conference held for the international press he was rather laconic. When asked about his personal life and preferences he simply made reference to his books: in them he had said all he wanted to say. As might be expected, there is no biography of Pär Lagerkvist, and he is not known to have encouraged scholars working in that direction. His first marriage ended in divorce. His second wife, Elaine, died in 1967. His son, Bengt Lagerkvist, is a well-known filmmaker.

Evening Land

Evening Land (Aftonland, 1953) was Pär Lagerkvist's ninth collection of poetry, and his thirty-sixth book. He was sixty-two at the time, and he had received many honors, including the Prize of the Nine (De Nios Pris, 1928) and the Bellman Prize (1945), two of the most distinguished Literary awards in Sweden. He had received an honorary doctorate from the University of Gothenburg (1941), had been elected a member of the Swedish Academy (1940), and had been awarded the Nobel Prize (1951), the year after his best known novel, *Barabbas,* appeared.

For an author like Lagerkvist, who through most of his writing career has been the great Questioner and Brooder—like his compatriots Viktor Rydberg (1828–1895) and August Strindberg (1849–1912)—it is entirely understandable that he should deal with questions of the meaning (or lack of meaning) of life, the fear of death, the existence (or non-existence) of god, and of man's belief (or failure to believe) in god. Even some selected titles of his books reflect such concerns: *Anguish* (1916), *Chaos* (1919), *The Eternal Smile* (1920), *Guest of Reality* (1925), *Vanquished Life* (1927), *Fighting Spirit* (1930), *The Man Without a Soul* (1936), the novels *Barabbas* (1950), *The Sibyl* (1956), *The Death of Ahasuerus* (1959), *Pilgrim at Sea* (1962), *The Holy Land* (1964) and *Marianne* (1967). It is not surprising that Lagerkvist at the age of sixty-two should consider the land of the evening, Evening Land, and ultimate questions, nor is it strange that in this book he would return, repeatedly, to childhood experiences. What are then some of the facts of his Childhood Land?

Childhood Land

Pär Lagerkvist was born on May 23, 1891, in the city of Växjö in the province of Småland, the southern part of Sweden. He was the last of seven children born to a railroad employee and his wife. His parents had moved from the country to the city only a few years earlier, and they kept up their contact with their country home to the extent that it was said of them that while living in the city, "they were more country folks than city dwellers." This was to be a significant fact in the young Pär's development. The attitudes of his parents were, by and large, traditional; their religion, especially that of Pär Lagerkvist's grandparents, almost identical with the old peasant religion, in which the Old Testament was dominant and was larded with bits of pietism. These farmers were generally suspicious of new ideas. They were not interested in international politics and hardly in national politics either; and if and when they voted, it was for the most conservative candidates. It is typical of Pär Lagerkvist's father that he refused to join the railroadmen's trade union, even though it meant losing a chance for a better salary.

Only on very rare occasions, in early works, Lagerkvist provided his readers with what is apparently "autobiographical" material. How does he characterize his home? "You don't often find such quiet in the world as there was in this home," he says in *Gäst hos verkligheten* (1925; trans. E. Mesterton and D. W. Harding, *Guest of Reality*, 1936). In the same book he gives a loving portrait of his mother: "Going about her jobs she was nearly always cheerful and used to like it if the big children had a joke about something, something she could listen to; but if she settled herself down for a rest she clasped her hands in her lap and gave a deep sigh and seemed to be far away from them all. In the evening she sat and read the Bible or the Prayer Book, not aloud, but whispering to herself."

In *Guest of Reality* Lagerkvist described his father in a less cheerful tone. When he came home in the evening, he put the signal lantern in the hallway, but only after having wiped it clean. After supper "he reached for the Bible and started reading. There was a strange heaviness when they both sat reading and no one spoke. The children kept quiet; it was so silent that they felt weighed down. . . . Sometimes when a late train arrived at the station the father went over to the window, stretched up and looked out, Bible in hand. Then he sat down again and went on reading."

In *Guest of Reality,* too, Lagerkvist has what might be taken as a description of himself as a child in the principal character, Anders. Anders is an unusual child. He is introspective and hypersensitive. His fears of death become obsessive thoughts which develop into compulsive actions, like visiting the ice-cellar or, on a rainy day, praying on a flat stone in the forest for the lives of everyone in the family. A boy who loved life as feverishly as he, would inevitably experience too the fear of the thing he hated the most—obliteration.

In the short story "Father and I" (*Onda sagor,* 1924; trans. M. Ekenberg, *Modern Swedish Short Stories,* London, 1934) Pär Lagerkvist tells of a walk in the forest that he, as a ten year old boy, took with his father. When dusk falls the boy is frightened by the fears he conjures up. He sees darkness everywhere and does not dare breathe deeply for fear that he will swallow too much darkness and therefore will have to die. He asks his father why it is so eerie when it is dark, and he gets the answer that it is not eerie. "After all we know that there is a God."

They travel on a trolley and then suddenly encounter an unannounced, extra train, a ghost train, and barely save their lives by jumping down onto the embankment. "What sort of train was it? There wasn't one due now! We gazed at it in terror. The fire blazed in the huge engine as they shoveled in coal; sparks whirled out into the night. It was terrible. The engineer stood there in the light of the fire, pale, motionless, his features as though turned to stone. Father didn't recognize him, didn't know who he was. The man just stared straight ahead, as though intent only on rushing into the darkness, far into the darkness that had no end."

In an epiphany the blazing locomotive engine is seen by the boy as a symbol of his—perhaps also of modern man's—future life: "But my whole body was shaking. It was for me, for my sake. I divined what it meant: it was the anguish that was to come, the unknown, all that Father knew nothing about, that he wouldn't be able to protect me against. That was how this world, this life, would be for me; not like Father's, where everything was secure and certain. It wasn't a real world, a real life. It just hurtled, blazing, into the darkness that had no end."

Even the portrait Lagerkvist draws of his maternal grandparents in his travelogue *Morgonen* ("The Morning," 1920; my translation) is relevant. While contemplating the difference between Southern and Northern ways of life, the narrator is suddenly seized by a memory from his earliest childhood

> when as a very small child I was out visiting on the old farm which was the family's real home. There lived an old woman, so old that it seemed somehow unreal to me. Once upon a time so far, far away that I could not comprehend it, she had borne my mother. Around that farm there always lay in the summer-time the fragrance of lavender and mignonette, and the great maple-trees were in bloom; but now it was winter. When at night the old woman would fetch water from the icy well, because the home was poor, she did not light a lantern, but from the sheaf of finely cut wood hanging down over the open hearth she took a long splinter and blew on the sparse embers, until it took fire; then she bit the other end of the stick with her teeth, and with the buckets in her hands she walked out into the pitch-black

night. I sat by the window, half frightened, looking. The fire fluttered beside her head, her thin, grey hair flew about, the red light flickered over the snow which lay buried in all the darkness out there.

The narrator also remembers

a scraggy old man who also lived on the farm where summer alternated with darkness and winter. He was my mother's father and a remarkable man. In his youth he existed only for God. His piety was deep and moving; one sensed from everything he did and said how filled he was with its warming light. But suddenly his life went astray. Something wild and hard, as though from ancient depths, appeared in him; he turned away from God, from his belief and everything; his life became a berserk rage against himself and what was his own, an evil darkness which I remember having earlier described as something incomprehensible. When he then became old, he returned to his God. And God received him as if nothing had happened. God received him as though he had merely been away for a short while, busy with living. He had known all the time that he would return again. It was then, when he had become old, that I first saw him. During those winter evenings, when the wind whizzed with whirling snow and nipping frost around the old farm, he used to sit close to the hearth reading in a loud voice from a Bible in which the words were larger than in any other I had seen. His hair was long and gray, and his face severe, his voice drowned out the storms outside; in the twilight the old woman stole about in stocking feet, sighing deeply. Frightened, I crouched in a faraway corner. I was afraid of their God. It was not the God we had at my mother's and father's home. I heard the wind howling as the old man turned a page; everything was frightful and dark; I thought they must be heathens.

* * *

A book of family sermons read in Pär Lagerkvist's home, and presumably even in his grandparents' home, contains this homily:

God wishes to maintain order and diversity among people in this world. – He himself has arranged the classes and without them the world cannot endure. The earthly advancement each of us ought to receive, God will let us experience in due time, without our doing anything about it. If he should let us stay in the lowly position where we stand, that is also according to His will, and we shall console ourselves with His grace and with the hope of eternal life.

Rebellion

This kind of teaching, essentially pleading for the *status quo,* went unheeded by Pär Lagerkvist. At school he had become acquainted with Darwin's theory of evolution, in which terms like "struggle," and "the natural selection" played such important parts. Darwin's theory opened up entirely new possibilities which his parents did not see but which he was determined to explore. Like the conservative farmers near Växjö, the bourgeois people of the city of Växjö were acutely sensitive to any departures from the *status quo.* To this inflexibility Pär Lagerkvist and four of his classmates, who called themselves "the Red Ring," answered by rebelling. In 1908/09 they held anarchist meetings on Sundays, at 11 A.M., exactly the time when the cathedral bells were summoning the community to service. The boys' radicalism was, however, largely apolitical and theoretical and, above all, it was concerned with religion. Among the books the young rebels discussed seem to have been those by Flammarion, Thomas Huxley, and Petr Kropotkin, as well as Strindberg's *Master Olof* and Ibsen's *Brand,* the latter two dramas about religious revolutionaries.

Pär Lagerkvist was thus intimately involved in the transition from the epoch of the old farming society to the new industrial one (which reached Sweden more than a century after its arrival in the United States and England). The experiences made necessary a break with his parents' religion.

Pär Lagerkvist rebelled against the oppressiveness of that religion, with its dogmatism and its rigidity, and became an "outsider," a stranger, at an early age.

The God Who May Not Even Exist

In *Evening Land* Lagerkvist's childhood experiences are a minor theme, a backdrop for the major theme, man's relationship with a god who may not even exist. This relationship is not without complications and ambiguities in Pär Lagerkvist's work. Especially if we were to take into account his total *oeuvre* with its involved transpositions and developments, the complexities would very soon become evident. Since most of Lagerkvist's poems remain untranslated, a few remarks limited to *Evening Land* will have to suffice in this context.

Did Lagerkvist write these poems over a very long span of time? Such a question is prompted by the manifest inconsistencies, turns and changes, and contradictions to be found in *Evening Land*. The remarkable thing is that, taken individually, each poem rings clear like a bell, and requires little or no commentary or explication, only some afterthought on the part of the reader. But when taken together as a whole, there is a cacophony of sounds, which is not so little bewildering. Sometimes god exists, sometimes he does not. Sometimes the poet-narrator is a believer, sometimes an agnostic. Now there is only absence of god, now the very same absence is "an even greater wonder," Pär Lagerkvist writes, for example. The poet's ambiguous hovering somewhere between two extremes—faith and lack of faith—is my sole excuse for tampering with these poems. In the process, readers who are unfamiliar with Lagerkvist's work should find a few useful hints for a reading, or better, a rereading of *Evening Land*.

It will be instructive to read in succession the last three poems in part IV, beginning with "Let my shadow disappear into yours. / Let me lose myself." It should perhaps be noted that "shadow" in the biblical Orient is something good: protection against the blazing sun. As we recall from Psalm 91: "He that dwelleth in the secret of the most High shall abide under the shadow of the Almighty." While the poet seems trusting, believing, and willing to surrender, or to be absorbed in god, ("let me lose myself"), in the next poem his relationship as a child to his father is indicated. But perhaps a child who had a strange religious experience from which he never recovered: "I only saw the world such as it is" (pp. 100–101). In almost existentialist terms it is stated that with or without a merciful father there will (perhaps!) be loneliness and darkness; with that insight, death and uncertainty is the one certain thing:

Hold me in your unknown hand,
and do not let go of me.
Carry me over morning-bright bridges,
and over the dizzy depths
where you keep darkness imprisoned.

But darkness can no longer be imprisoned.
Soon it will be evening over your bridges,
then night.
And perhaps I shall be very lonely.

In the final poem of this group, the outsider, the individualist and rebel, never far away in Lagerkvist, perceives man's *fight* against anxiety, loneliness, alienation, death wishes, suffering and despair as something in itself positive and meaningful, perhaps because it compels man to attempt to transcend himself, in dreams, imagination, religion, creative work:

May my heart's disquiet never vanish.

May I never be at peace.
May I never be reconciled to life, nor to death either.
May my path be unending, with death its unknowable goal.

To be sure the poem is a prayer to someone, but at the same
time it is a declaration of independence, even of a certain
defiance. The three poems above exemplify the wide range of
attitudes in *Evening Land.*

The Wanderer

From the very beginning of *Evening Land* and throughout
the entire collection, the theme of the *wanderer, wandering,*
is employed: "It is in the evening that one breaks up / at
sunset. . . . The desert wanderer abandons his camp-site." and
the wanderer is part of what holds *Evening Land* together.
But the wanderer is no ordinary wanderer. He seems to shift
character. Sometimes he appears to be man alive (or dead),
sometimes death, and sometimes god or gods.

In the childhood memory eternalized in a poem such as
"With old eyes I look back" (pp. 110–111) the wanderer is
obviously the poet-narrator:

My soul has been chosen to search far away
for hidden things, to wander under stars.

The wanderer who "existed before the mountains and the
clouds" (pp. 88–89), "who eternally young wandered among
the stars of the Milky Way" may be cosmic and *divine,* yet
sharing a *human* quality, desolation:

you who were alone before loneliness,
and whose heart was full of disquiet before any human heart—

When this wanderer's mere shadow fell over the earth (pp. 96—97) the shadow miraculously acted as "a strong light" which awakened the people in the tents. —Partly interwoven with the theme of the wanderer is that of the *stranger,* which appears in Parts IV and V of *Evening Land.*

The Stranger

A stranger am I, was a stranger born.
A stranger even in the autumn of my life.

A look at the word *stranger* and its relatives *estrangier* and *extraneus,* "he who is without," makes it easy to connect with an outsider, and here, more precisely, with someone who persists as an outsider even in old age. As a mere boy an overwhelming experience caused him to lose his childhood innocence ("It was then that for the first time I saw the stars. / ... / I stood there absolutely still. And everything vanished for me, . . ." [pp. 104—105]). It is symbolic that when he has come indoors, he sat down on his footstool "far away from the others," like someone who does not belong, or someone who must be apart from the others. To the one who considers himself "chosen," and assumes that there was once made a mysterious sign "on his childhood window" everything in the world suddenly "seemed so strange" (pp. 100—101). Barabbas, the Sibyl, and Ahasuerus in Lagerkvist's novels are such "chosen" ones, outsiders, loners, doubters; and so are a number of "saviours" (in *The Eternal Smile;* "Saviour John," the hero in "A Hero's Death" in *Evil Tales,* and the hero in the play *The Invisible One*) and those who identify with a negative "saviour" such as the Dwarf, and medieval man's scapegoat, the Hangman. It can be argued that Anders in *Guest of Reality* is chosen to see "the world such as it is," and yet to have an eternal longing.

The "stranger" in the poem, opening *Evening Land,* IV,

according to Kai Henmark, may be the god "whom Pär Lagerkvist will fear the longest, namely death":

I should like to be someone else
but I don't know who.
A stranger stands with his back to me, his forehead
facing the burning home of the stars.
I shall never meet his eyes,
never see his features.

I should like to be someone else
a stranger, other than myself.

In Lagerkvist's *Guest of Reality,* to the main character, Anders, God and death are intertwined concepts. On the one hand death, or, the fear of death, can bring man closer to God. On the other hand, one of God's attributes, such as thunder, can cause death and destruction through lightning. ("It's good hearing it thunder, then you know for sure that God is in power," said the grandfather in *Guest of Reality.*)

Lagerkvist's *stranger* is a shape-shifter like the *wanderer.* Sometimes the stranger tends to look like a "saviour," at other times like god, or death. As Kai Henmark has pointed out, "the stranger becomes all this and in different degrees, but in all his appearances he had his origin in the poet's childhood. Under the influence of the stranger—childhood god, the poet transforms himself into a stranger, and becomes an equal to god. Literally in the name of god he can talk of the feeling of loss, when the young bird leaves its nest—god and man are easily mistaken for the other, filled with longing, yet impartial:"

I am the hand from which the fledgeling flew,
the hand of the creator.

It will never return to me,
to its nest.
Nothing returns to me.

Pp. 164–165

In the poem above Lagerkvist thus uses the *persona* of god, and it is worth noticing that *god* appears *lonely* or disappointed at his creation, just as in another poem describing the land of death (pp. 58–59) *man* feels abandoned and *lonely:*

They all have fled, all my friends,
the summer wind, the dewy grass in the morning,
the fragrance in the forest after rain. I am all alone.
All the fountains of life
have fallen silent.
Abandoned, abandoned.

Purpose of Shape-shifting?

What might be Lagerkvist's purpose with such shape-shifting in the "wanderer" and "the stranger–god" as mentioned before? Is it not to suggest that the human and the divine are intertwined forever? It will be clearer if we compare with *Sibyllan* (1956; trans N. Walford, *The Sibyl,* 1958) in which Lagerkvist makes the main protagonist define *her* (and presumably also *his*) view that the divine is conspicuously multi-faceted:

> God is merciless. Those who say he is good do not know him. He is the most inhuman thing there is. He is as wild and incalculable as lightning. Like lightning out of a cloud which one did not know contained lightning. Suddenly it strikes, suddenly he strikes down on one, revealing all his cruelty. Or his love–his cruel love. With

him anything may happen. He reveals himself at any time and in anything. . . . The divine is not human; it is something quite different. And it is not noble or sublime or spiritualized, as one likes to believe. It is alien and repellent and sometimes it is madness. It is malignant and dangerous and fatal. Or so I have found it. . . .

And as far as I can understand, he is both evil and good, both light and darkness, both meaningless and full of meaning which we can never perceive, yet never cease to puzzle over. A riddle which is intended not to be solved but to exist. To exist for us always. To trouble us always. . . .

He has made me very unhappy. But he has also allowed me to know a happiness passing all understanding. He has, and I must not forget that. . . . What would my life have been without him? If I had never been filled with him, with his spirit? If I had never felt the bliss that poured from him, the anguish and pain that is his also, and the wonder of being annihilated in his blazing arms, of being altogether his? Of feeling his rapture, his boundless bliss, and sharing god's infinite happiness in being alive?

The human and the divine and everything else appear intertwined to an extent that is not always fully realized.

Religious Experiences

Various kinds of religious experience are described by Lagerkvist in Part IV of *Evening Land*. The all-exclusive character of an *unio mystica* (or an approximation thereof) is evident from this poem:

Throw open your house to me,
open all doors and gates to me,
as I enter like a storm wind.

When I march in, there will no longer be any room for you,
you shall dwell in the desert as an outcast.
I shall drive you out into the desert,
you shall lie naked in the desert under the stars.

But in the house which has been yours I shall live,
I shall fill it with my presence.

It should be noted that the Hebrew word "nefesh" stands for "spirit," "wind," thus suggesting that the "storm wind" is also "god." God in these poems is sometimes described as a fire: "Others burn in your fire, rest in your burning arms," (pp. 120–121) and in the lines: "You touched me / and I became ashes./ My ego, my self turned to ashes, consumed by you" (pp. 134–135). In Deuteronomy 4:24 the image of God as fire is found in the expression: "For the Lord thy God is a consuming fire, even a jealous God."

There are also examples of low-keyed religious experiences, like a drawn-out inspiration, consisting of vague and undefined longings, feelings of emptiness and loneliness, which in their turn may give birth to the thought (later the conviction) that god may not exist at all:

The god who does not exist,
he it is who enkindles my soul,
who makes my soul into a wilderness,
a reeking ground, a scorched land, reeking after a fire.
Because he does not exist.
He it is who saves my soul by making it a desert
and scorched.
The god who does not exist,
the awesome god.

This thought is further developed in the next poem (pp. 124–125):

It is not god who loves us, it is we who love him,
who reach out for him in longing after something else,
someone greater than ourselves,
as love does.
And our longing becomes the more intense the less it is
    returned,
our despair the deeper the more we realize that we are
    deserted,
that we are loved by no one.

What is deeper than absence, than unreturned love?

The idea that god in fact is "*our* mysterious work," Lagerkvist put forward already in 1912, and in 1920, in the previously quoted travelogue, "The Morning" (which ties it to the cycle "The Morning of Creation"). A similar thought was expressed by American humanists of the 1880s and 1890s.

A "Reversal" of the Creative Process

The poet thus "reverses" the creative process: we humans invented god, not the other way around. But paradoxically:

If you believe in god and there is no god
then your belief is an even greater wonder.
Then it is really something inconceivably great.

In Lagerkvist's work, faith and substitutes for faith, such as religious symbols or trappings tend to substitute for god as the focus of devotion (cf. Kai Henmark). Judging from the poem about the spear-caster (pp. 128–131), it is Lagerkvist's contention that the force of that faith, represented by the spear-caster, originated nowhere except within man himself. However, in an apparent ironic twist against himself Lagerkvist in the final stanza asks, "Why is that not enough for you?" (i.e., acceptance of a god as something necessary and entirely human, even in the most extraordinary times).

In the final suite, "The Morning of Creation" (pp. 149–165), Lagerkvist takes on the *personae* of the Creator and some of his creations, such as a fledgling bird, flowers, a cloud, the sky, the dark star Earth, man, the stars. The first and last poem is in the *persona* of God himself, who (characteristically) longs for fellowship. *Evening Land* ends with a picture of the Brooder and Questioner wondering: "Why do I still sit here on the shore which he left so long ago?" thus indicating that the paradoxical connection between god and man continues to be in effect, although it may exist only as man's wish.

It should be clear even from these brief comments on the poems of *Evening Land* that Pär Lagerkvist's attempt to resolve the delicate, paradoxical relationship between man and a (non-existent) god, remains at best unresolved, and uncertain. In this respect Lagerkvist's attitude is thoroughly modern. What kind of redemption does this leave us? The narrator-poet's often mentioned *longing* probably implies that *love, the fulfilment of human contact,* is the answer to man's problems.

In his "humanist manifesto," *Den knutna näven* (The Clenched Fist, 1934), Pär Lagerkvist wrote, "I am a believer without a faith, a religious atheist. I understand Gethsemane, but not the jubilation over the victory." It can safely be assumed that Lagerkvist when writing *Evening Land* remained basically non-confessional and non-dogmatic, and

that he felt compelled to develop his peculiar, personal be-
liefs as a "religious atheist."

Symbols

The desert, the desert wanderer (cf. Lagerkvist's *Barabbas*),
the last darkness (cf. Anders's fear of death in Lagerkvist's
Guest of Reality), the stars and constellations, etc., which
appear in *Evening Land* are familiar symbols to readers of Pär
Lagerkvist's earlier writings. It would, however, require a very
substantial and lengthy study to determine the shifts in
meaning of these and other symbols, and their interrelation-
ships in Lagerkvist's entire *oeuvre*. What can be briefly
pointed to here is how the poet, almost magically, alternates
between two levels: one in which man experiences god on an
expanding cosmic scale, the other in which man, existentially
alone and deserted, experiences *gudstanken,* the idea of god,
in narrow, personal terms. The latter experience presents
itself in loneliness and longing:

O galaxy above the soul's loneliness
o eternal longing
Pp. 80–81

The loneliness and "eternal longing" (implying "endless longing," as well as "longing for the eternal"), together with
anguish and irresoluteness, the poet hints, constitute the basis
of our religion and religious needs. (Cf. Kai Henmark,
Främlingen Lagerkvist, p. 26). Once the *idea* of god has
received a foothold in man's mind, the very *idea* functions
much the same way as the spear-point in the poem about the
spear-caster (pp. 128–131). As Henmark has shown, the spear
is Pär Lagerkvist's image for the *idea of god,* which in itself is

39

eternal, as long as "unborn hearts wait to be pierced by it." It is thus Lagerkvist's contention that eternal questions will continue to occupy new minds. Already in a brief prose sketch, published in the Socialist magazine *Fram,* 1912, Lagerkvist had expounded a similar idea: A young hunter catches a glimpse of a woman by a spring. His feelings are aroused, but in such a contradictory way that, simultaneously, he is attracted to her and yet wants to withdraw from her. Compulsively he has to search for her or follow her, sometimes close by, sometimes remotely, sometimes when she is out of sight. Once she again reappears at the spring and he wants to kiss her—it is his own image that he kisses on the surface of the water. He discovers that he is completely alone. The phantasy is called *Gudstanken:* the idea of god.

If the thought of god appears, disappears, and appears again, like a flickering light or like the woman of that prose piece and so many other works of Lagerkvist's, his feelings of *longing* for the divine have dominated. If his *reason* is allowed to dominate, as it does most often in Lagerkvist's work, god is done away with or presents himself merely as an obsessive thought of man himself, and man, therefore, becomes god's father, as it were.

It is quite obvious from Lagerkvist's *Guest of Reality* how powerful Darwinism worked on the main protagonist's mind. "No, the teaching which one gets rubbed into himself [at school], *it* swept away God and all hope, *it* laid life open and raw, in all its nakedness, all its systematic meaninglessness, *it* was better, it helped. And it was true. No faith—just things as they are." Without going into detail about Lagerkvist's ideas of evolution, it is interesting to recall that in *Det besegrade livet* (Vanquished life, 1927, here in my translation) Lagerkvist applied evolution to the concept of god:

> Behold man, the creator of god (*gudamodern*)! Himself risen from the amoeba, from the protozoans of the sea, man projects heavens over the earth, he creates radiant multitudes of gods, which he leads through the heavens to rule over everything.

He dreams to himself eternity, because life is not enough for him. He creates sublime forms, almighty, eternal beings, because his soul hungers for perfection. . . .
  What if all these ideas of God, all these eschatological visions (evighetssyner), which nonetheless are to be found only within ourselves, all these mighty creations of religion were merely prophecies of what will come some day as fullest reality. . . .
  If we ought to say in humbleness and quiet assurance: God does not yet exist, but when we will be fully worthy of him, then he will come. Not from the outside, but from ourselves. And he shall reign within us and penetrate everything with his light. All spheres, all things, transforming, transfiguring them [förvandlande, förklarande dem].

A parallel thought has, incidentally, been expressed by Simone Weil in *La pesanteur et la grâce* (1947; trans. E. Craufurd as *Gravity and Grace*, 1952).

It is, of course, only for future scholarship to establish whether Lagerkvist remained faithful to views expressed in *Vanquished Life,* when writing *Evening Land,* which, after all, was composed more than a quarter century later, but one has the feeling that he stayed on the same course, only evolving new, ever more intricate aspects of his theme. In fact, it can be maintained that Lagerkvist more vigorously than anyone else in Scandinavia has explored religious concerns of both the modern heretic, influenced by natural science, and the modern brooder-searcher, desperately *wanting* to believe in the traditional religious values. In this the poet Pär Lagerkvist is unique.

A point of explication should be made regarding the symbol of the star, as Lagerkvist uses it in the poem "With old eyes I look back," (pp. 110–113) speaking, mysteriously, of the old country family:

They also lived in the light of a lonely star

when their heavy working day was over.
Together they sat in its quiet light
the light of a single star—not of all, of all.

By "the light of a single star" Lagerkvist might mean that the entire old family accepted *one* prescribed, uncomplicated god, that is, according to the dogma of their time. To the young, more modern "outsider" (of the poem) the idea of life, or god, is otherwise, and enormously complex. It is not like *one* star, but a myriad of stars, each with a multitude of intriguing facets, and for that reason less completely acceptable, because they are neither fully comprehensible nor believable.

Bibliography

Edfelt, Johannes. "Svensk lyrik." Stockholm, 1947.

Edman, Gunnar. "Pär Lagerkvists Credo." *Horisont* (Oslo, 1957), pp. 209–13.

Henmark, Kai. *Främlingen Lagerkvist.* Stockholm: Tema, Rabén & Sjögren, 1966.

Lagerkvist, Pär. *Prosa (Det besegrade livet).* Stockholm: Bonniers, 1945.

Lagerkvist, Pär. *The Eternal Smile and Other Stories.* Introduction by Richard B. Vowles. New York: Random House, 1953.

Malmström, Gunnel. *Menneskehjertets verden: Hovedmotiv i Pär Lagerkvists diktning.* Oslo: Gyldendal Norsk Forlag, 1970.

Linder, Erik Hjalmar. *Fem decennier av nittonhundratalet,* vol. 1. Stockholm: Natur och kultur, 1965.

Oberholzer, Otto. *Pär Lagerkvist.* Heidelberg: Carl Winter-Universitätsverlag, 1958.

Ryberg, Anders. *Pär Lagerkvist in Translation. A Bibliography.* Stockholm: Bonniers, 1964.

Skartveit, Andreas. *Gud skapt i menneskets bilete: Ein Lagerkviststudie.* Oslo: Det norske samlaget, 1966.

Willers, Uno. *Pär Lagerkvist Bibliografi.* Stockholm: Bonniers, 1951.

I

Det är om aftonen man bryter upp,
vid solnedgången.
Det är då man lämnar allt.

Tanken tar ner sina tält av spindelväv
och hjärtat glömmer varför det ängslats.
Ökenvandraren överger sin lägerplats,
som snart skall utplånas av sanden,
och fortsätter sin färd i nattens stillhet,
ledd av gåtfulla stjärnor.

It is in the evening that one breaks up,
at sunset.
Then it is that one abandons everything.

Mind takes down its tents of spider-web,
and heart forgets why it felt anxious.
The desert wanderer abandons his camp site,
which soon will be obliterated by the sand,
and continues on his journey in the stillness of the night,
guided by mysterious stars.

Vid färdens sista rast, i aftonhuset,
där bryts ett bröd och ätes under tystnad
i skymningsljus från fönstrets skumma ruta.

Det tänds ej någon lampa där för natten,
för ingen lampas olja skulle räcka,
och inget stamp av hästar skall dig väcka
för att en gäst skall vidare i natten.

Långt borta är det morgon över träden
och blommor öppnas för att livet smycka,
men du har glömt dem, blommorna och träden,
vad som var jordisk sorg och jordisk lycka.

At the journey's last halt, in the house of evening,
bread is broken and eaten in silence,
as twilight shines dimly through the window pane.

No lamp is lit for the night,
for no oil would suffice,
and no stamping of horses will wake you up
for a guest who departs in the night.

Far away morning dawns over the trees,
and flowers open to adorn life,
but you have forgotten both the trees and the flowers,
all earthly grief and earthly good-fortune.

(R)

Engång skall du vara en av dem som levat för längesen.
Jorden skall minnas dig så som den minns gräset och skogarna,
det multnade lövet.
Så som myllan minns
och så som bergen minns vindarna.
Din frid skall vara oändlig så som havet.

Some day you will be one of those who lived long ago.
The earth will remember you, just as it remembers the grass
                                        and the forests,
the rotting leaves.
Just as the soil remembers,
and just as the mountains remember the winds.
Your peace shall be as unending as that of the sea.

DEN DÖDE

Allting finns, blott jag ej längre finnes,
allt är kvar, den lukt av regn i gräset
som jag minns och vindens sus i träden,
molnens flykt och mänskohjärtats oro.

Blott mitt hjärtas oro finns ej längre.

THE DEAD ONE

All is there, only I am no more,
all is still there, the fragrance of rain in the grass
as I remember it, and the sough of wind in the trees,
the flight of the clouds and the disquiet of the human heart.

Only my heart's disquiet is no longer there.

(R)

Allt skall glömmas. Alla mänskoöden
stiga nedför glömskans skumma trappsteg
för att slockna i det sista mörkret.
Allt skall slockna. Tragedien sluta,
rampen släckas, himlens alla stjärnor
som bevittnat dramats grymma handling,
meningslös och fattig i sin ondska.
Scenen tom, med sjaskiga kulisser,
och den lilla giftdolk mänskor använt
mot varandra bortslängd i sin skräphög.

Glömska, tystnad. Ingenting att minnas.
Ingen som kan minnas.
Tomhet.

Var det allt?
Det vet vi inte.

All will become forgotten. All human fates
walk down the unlit stairs of oblivion
to go out into the final darkness.
All lights will be quenched. The tragedy end,
the footlights be put out, all the stars of heaven
that witnessed the drama's cruel action,
meaningless and paltry in its evil.
The stage and its shabby back-stage both empty,
and the little poison dagger the characters have used
against each other thrown away onto the rubbish heap.

Oblivion, silence. Nothing to remember.
No one who can remember.
Emptiness.

Was that all?
That we do not know.

II

Skuggor skrider genom mina riken,
slocknade ljusgestalter.

Bergen lyfter sina öde tinnar.
Det är aska på dem efter eldar.

Fågellöst, övergivet land. Vem levde engång här?

Slocknade facklor bärs genom dalar,
genom tomma dalar.
Facklor som förlorat sin låga i rymdens tomhet,
i en rymd utan morgon och afton.

Shadows glide through my lands,
quenched shapes of light.

The moutains raise their desolate summits.
There are ashes upon them, following fires.

Birdless deserted regions. Who once lived here?

Extinguished torches are born through valleys,
empty valleys.
Torches whose flames have been quenched in the emptiness
of space,
a space without morning or evening.

Övergiven av morgonhimlen och stjärnorna,
av sommargräset och det friska vårregnet,
av alla det levandes källsprång.
Övergiven.

Alla har de flytt, alla mina vänner,
sommarvinden, det daggiga gräset om morgonen,
lukten i skogen efter regnet, jag är alldeles ensam.
Alla det levandes källor
har tystnat.
Övergiven, övergiven.

Var går vägen till mörkret, det barmhärtiga, mjuka?
Var är utgångsporten i muren kring livets land,
den låga, där man böjer sig ner?

Abandoned by the morning sky and the stars,
the grass of summer and the fresh spring rain,
by all the fountains of life.
Abandoned.

They all have fled, all my friends,
the summer wind, the dewy grass in the morning,
the fragrance in the forest after rain. I am all alone.
All the fountains of life
have fallen silent.
Abandoned, abandoned.

Whither leads the way into darkness, the soft, the merciful?
Where is the exit in the wall around the land of Life,
the low-roofed exit where one must duck one's head?

I ökenlandet, vid det dödas sjö,
i ensamhetens månlandskap — —

Vad har min tanke att göra vid dessa saltstränder.
Varför svävar min själ över denna gråa vattenspegel
som har blyets och likens färg.

Rop skulle höras. Men hörs inte.
Tält skulle tas ner, kameler lastas i gryningen.

Men allt är tystnad.
Öknen närmar sig försiktigt med sin döda strand
och det orörliga vattnet rör sig inte.
Bara min själ svävar över dess spetälskegråa yta
på outtröttliga trötta vingar.

In the desert beside the Sea of the Dead,
in the lunar landscape of loneliness —

What have my thoughts to do with these salt beaches?
Why does my soul hover over this mirror of grey water,
the color of lead and ashes?

Cries should be heard, but are not heard,
tents be taken down, camels loaded at daybreak.

But all is silence.
Cautiously the dead shore of the desert moves forward,
but the motionless water does not move.
Only my soul hovers over its leprous surface
on tireless tired wings.

Omgiven av tomhet
så som en stjärnbild av rymden,
med oändliga avstånd mellan sina ljuspunkter,
mellan de tidlösa uppenbarelserna av sig själv.

Så lever i fullkomlig jämvikt,
i död fulländning,
Sanningen om det stora Intet.
Tomhetens själ.

Så som en stjärnbild
med en bortglömd gudomlighets namn.

Surrounded by a void,
as a constellation is by space,
with infinite distance between its luminous points,
its timeless manifestations of itself.

So in complete calm,
in dead perfection,
lives the Truth about the great Nothing.
The soul of the void.

Like a constellation
named after an utterly forgotten divinity.

III

Jag ville veta
men fick bara fråga,
jag ville ljus
men fick bara brinna.
Jag begärde det oerhörda
och fick bara leva.

Jag beklagade mig.
Men ingen förstod vad jag mente.

I wanted to know
but was only allowed to ask,
I wanted light
but was only allowed to burn.
I demanded the ineffable
but was only allowed to live.

I complained,
but nobody understood what I meant.

O människa, du brunn där stjärnor speglas.
Hur ofta stod jag inte och såg ner i djupet
och sökte tyda gåtans dubbla mening.
Hur ofta ville jag ej dricka klarhet, visshet
ur detta icke rena, djupa vatten,
så lämpligt till att spegla stjärnor på sin yta,
men inte till att lindra själens törst och vånda.

Din dryck är unken och ditt djup är grumligt
och stjärnans ljus hos dig är bara lånat.
Och ändå — hela stjärnevalvets gåta
är ingenting mot gåtan i din spegel.

O Man, O well where stars are mirrored.
How often have I stood and looked down into your depths,
trying to solve the double meaning of your riddle.
How often have I wanted to drink clarity, certainty,
from your deep but unclean water,
so able to mirror stars on its surface
but not to sooth the thirst and agony of the soul.

Your water is stale, your depth impure,
the starlight in you is only borrowed.
and yet—the riddle of the whole firmament
is nothing beside the riddle in your mirror.

(R)

Du människa som står vid stranden av mig,
lyss till min sång.
Lyss till en liten liten del av min sång,
min eviga sång
mot stranden.

Gå inte din väg. Vänd dig inte bort.
Du förströr mig med din närvaro
som jag förströr dig med mina vågors sorl.
Du främmande, du vars ansikte är så vackert tillfälligt.

Varför gör jag dig sorgsen?
Varför blir ditt ansikte så svårmodigt av min sång,
av det evigas sång,
av vågornas sång
mot stranden?
Varför bedrövar jag dig?

O Man who stands beside my shore,
listen to my song.
Listen to a little bit of my song,
my eternal song
against the shore.

Do not go on your way. Do not turn away.
You amuse me with your presence,
as I amuse you with the murmurings of my waves.
O stranger, whose face is so beautifully accidental.

Why do I make you sad?
Why does your face look so melancholy as I sing,
the song of the eternal,
the song of the waves
against the shore?
Why do I distress you?

Min längtan är inte min.
Den är gammal så som stjärnorna.
Född ur Intet engång
som de,
ur den gränslösa tomheten.

Suset i träden,
vågens slag mot stranden,
de stora bergen långt borta —
de väcker min längtan.
Men inte till någonting här.
Till något oändligt långt borta,
någonting för länge länge sen —

Långt före havet, långt före bergen, långt före vindarna —

My longing is not my own.
It is just as old as the stars.
Once born like them
out of Nothing,
out of the boundless void.

The murmur in the trees,
the beating of the wave against the shore,
the tall mountains far away —
they arouse my longing.
But not to anything here.
To something infinitely far away,
something long long ago —

Long before the sea, long before the mountains, long before
the winds —

Jag lyssnar till vinden som sopar igen mina spår.
Vinden som ingenting minns
och som inte alls förstår eller bryr sig om vad den gör,
men som är så vacker att lyssna till.
Den mjuka vinden,
mjuk som glömskan.

När den nya morgonen gryr
skall jag vandra vidare.
I den vindstilla gryningen skall jag börja vandringen
på nytt
med det allra första steget
i den underbart orörda sanden.

I listen to the wind that obliterates my traces.
The wind that remembers nothing,
understands nothing nor cares what it does,
but is so lovely to listen to.
The soft wind,
soft like oblivion.

When the new morning breaks
I shall wander further,
in the windless dawn begin my wandering afresh
with my very first step
in the wonderfully untouched sand.

Där vandrar fjärran på blåa stigar
med huvud krönta av silverkronor
gestalter höga som ingen skådat —

Där lyfter konungar kungakronan
och okänt ljus i dess stenar glimmar
och allt är morgon och första gång,
en evig morgon och soluppgång.

Far off on blue paths,
heads crowned with silver,
wander tall forms that no one has beheld —

There kings lift their kingly crowns
in the stones of which glimmers a mystic light:
all is morning and for the first time,
eternal morning and sunrise.

Då bryts murarna ner
av oerhörda änglar
och frihet, frihet förkunnas
för alla själar,
för min själ,
för din själ.
Då brister alla bojor
vid en svindlande hög ton,
så hög att ingen kan höra den,
men vi ser bojorna brista som kristall.
Då är fullkomningens tidsålder inne,
och alla himlar blir fulla av frid,
de rasade murarnas frid,
de stigande rymdernas frid,
frihetens frid
utan all gräns.

Then the walls will be broken down
by gigantic angels
and freedom, freedom be proclaimed
to all souls,
to mine,
to yours.
Then all fetters shall be broken asunder
with a sound giddy and shrill,
so shrill that none can hear it,
but we see the fetters cracking like crystals.
Then the age of perfection will be at hand,
and all the heavens filled with peace,
the peace of razed walls,
the peace of the ascending heavens,
the peace of freedom
without end.

Du vintergata över själens ensamhet,
du eviga längtan.
Brinn, brinn långt efter mig,
långt efter att jag inte finns,
jag som aldrig fick bestiga din bro.
Brinn för det folk som skall komma vandrande engång
genom rymderna,
som skall vandra tryggt över avgrunden på en bro
av stjärnor.

O galaxy above the soul's loneliness,
O eternal longing.
Burn, burn long after me,
long after I no longer exist,
I who was never permitted to climb your bridge.
Burn for those who shall come walking some day
                    through the planetary spaces,
wandering safely across the abyss on a bridge
                              of stars.

IV

Jag ville vara en annan,
men jag vet inte vem.
En främling står bortvänd, med pannan
mot stjärnornas lågande hem.
Jag skall aldrig se hans ögon
och aldrig hans anletsdrag.

Jag ville vara en annan,
en främling, en annan än jag.

I should like to be somebody else,
but I don't know who.
A stranger stands with his back to me, his forehead
facing the burning home of the stars.
I shall never meet his eyes,
never see his features.

I should like to be somebody else,
a stranger, other than myself.

Jag är den som fortsätter
när du dröjer kvar,
som stiger ut i natten
när du går till vila.
Som öppnar porten till mörkret
och går vidare,
till mörkret och stjärnorna
och går vidare.
På en oviss stig,
en stig som kanske inte alls finns,
överger jag dig.

I am the one who goes on
when you remain behind,
the one who steps out into the night
when you retire to rest.
The one who opens the gate into the darkness
and walks further
into the darkness and the stars
and walks further.
On an uncertain path,
a path which perhaps does not exist,
I forsake you.

Du som fanns före bergen och molnen,
före havet och vindarna.
Du vars begynnelse är före alla tings begynnelse
och vars glädje och sorg är äldre än stjärnorna.
Du som har vandrat evigt ung över vintergator
och genom de stora mörkren mellan dem.
Du som var ensam före ensamheten
och vars hjärta var fullt av ängslan långt före något
                              mänskohjärta —
glöm inte mig.

Men hur skulle du kunna minnas mig.
Hur skulle havet kunna minnas havssnäckan
som det brusade igenom engång.

You who existed before the mountains and the clouds,
before the sea and the winds.
You whose beginning is before the beginning of all things,
and whose joy and sorrow are older than the stars.
You who eternally young wandered among the stars of the
                                                    Milky Way
and through the great darknesses between them.
You who were alone before loneliness,
and whose heart was full of disquiet before any human heart —

do not forget me.

But how could you possibly remember me?
How could the sea possibly remember the sea-shell
that once it surged through.

Tillfällig som en vallmo, som vecket i en vandrandes kläder,
en okänd vandrare
med ett okänt mål.

Vem är jag?

Som ett grässtrås böjning i vinden.
När det reser sig igen har ingenting hänt,
ingenting som helst.

Men vem är han, vandraren?
Han som inte är tillfällig som jag.
Jag frågar. Men hur skulle han kunna förklara det för mig?

Obegripligt är mig allting
under en himmel fullskriven med stjärnor.

An accident like a poppy or the crease in a wanderer's clothes,
an unknown wanderer
with a nameless goal.

Who am I?

Like a grass-blade bending before the wind
When it raises its head again, nothing has happened,
nothing at all.

But who is he, who is the wanderer,
who is not an accident like me.
I ask. But how could he ever explain this to me?

Under a sky, scribbled all over with stars,
everything is incomprehensible.

Vem har gått före mig här och ristat alla dessa tecken
                                        på himlen?
Jag förstår inte hans skrift, men kanske menar han att jag
                                        skall följa honom.
Varthän?

Inte kan jag skrida fram igenom rymderna
som han.
Jag måste stanna här där jag antagligen hör hemma
— säker på det kan man ju inte vara.
Jag måste stanna under de tecken han händelsevis ristat
                                        just här
på sin väg genom de oändliga rymderna,
tecken som kanske inte alls betyder att man skall följa honom
Fast säker kan man ju aldrig vara.

Who has walked here before me and inscribed these signs
                                on the firmament?
I do not understand his writing, but perhaps he means I
                                should follow him.
Whither?

I cannot glide through space
like him.
I have to stay where, presumably, I belong,
but of that one can never be certain.
I have to remain under the signs which he accidentally
                                inscribed just here
on his way through the infinite spaces,
signs which perhaps don't mean at all that I should follow him,
though, of course, one can never be certain.

Av det som för honom bara var en lägerplats för natten
vill jag och de mina göra oss en grotta
och leva och dö där,
för troligtvis är detta meningen med oss.
Och hans obegripliga tecken i valvet skall ge grottan frid.
Så är vårt hopp. Att vandringsmannens oro skall bli vår frid.
Men härom vet vi ju ingenting.

Out of what to him was only a resting-place for the night
I and mine will make ourselves a cave
to live and die in,
for, most likely, that is what he intends with us.
And his incomprehensible signs in the heavens shall give peace
                                                    to the cave.
Such is our hope: that the wanderer's disquiet shall become
                                            our peace.
But, of course, we know nothing about this.

Hans skugga föll över jorden.
Gick han förbi ute i stjärnljuset?
Förbi vår boplats på väg till någonting annat än vi?
Hans skugga föll över våra tält
och vi vaknade i natten som av ett starkt sken.

Hans skugga är inte han,
men det blev ljust i tälten.

Den natten kunde vi inte sova mer.

His shadow fell across the earth.
Did he walk past in the starlight?
Past our dwelling-place on his way to something other than us?
His shadow fell across our tents,
and we awoke in the night as if woken by a strong light.

He is not his shadow,
but his shadow became light in our tents.

That night we could sleep no more.

Vem gick förbi min barndoms fönster
och andades på det,
vem gick förbi i den djupa barndomsnatten,
som ännu inte har några stjärnor.

Med sitt finger gjorde han ett tecken på rutan,
på den immiga rutan,
med det mjuka av sitt finger,
och gick vidare i sina tankar.
Lämnade mig övergiven
för evigt.

Hur skulle jag kunna tyda tecknet,
tecknet i imman efter hans andedräkt.
Det stod kvar en stund, men inte tillräckligt länge för att
jag skulle kunna tyda det.
Evigheters evighet skulle inte ha räckt till för att tyda det.

Who walked past the window of my childhood
and breathed on it?
Who walked past in the deep night of childhood,
that still was starless?

With his finger he made a sign on the pane,
on the moist pane
with the ball of his finger,
and then passed on to think of other things,
leaving me deserted
for ever.

How should I be able to interpret the sign,
the sign in the moist afterwards of his breath?
It stayed there a while, but not long enough
for me to be able to interpret it.
For ever and ever would not have sufficed to interpret it.

När jag steg upp om morgonen var fönsterrutan alldeles
klar
och jag såg bara världen sådan som den är.
Allt var mig så främmande i den
och min själ var full av ensamhet och ängslan bakom rutan.

Vem gick förbi,
förbi i den djupa barndomsnatten
och lämnade mig övergiven
för evigt.

When I got up in the morning, the window-pane was
                                    entirely clear,
and I only saw the world such as it is.
Everything in it seemed so strange to me,
and, behind the pane, my soul was filled with loneliness
                                    and longing.

Who walked past,
walked past in the deep night of childhood,
leaving me deserted
for ever.

Överallt, i alla himlar finner du hans spår,
alla rymder är fyllda av hans hemliga tecken,
alla höjder, alla djup av hans skrift, som han bara själv
kan tyda.

O väldige, varför lär du oss inte läsa din bok.
Varför för du inte ditt finger utefter tecknen
och lär oss stava och förstå så som barn.

Nej, det gör du inte. Någon skolmästare är du inte.
Du låter det vara så som det är. Obegripligt så som
det är.

Och engång i tidernas afton, skall du då stryka ut allt-
sammans igen
och låta allting bli mörker, så som det var innan du reste
dig ur dina tankar
och vandrade bort för att uppteckna dem på din väg
med det glödande kolet i din hand?

Everywhere, in all the heavens you will find his footprints,
all regions are filled with his mysterious letters,
all heights and depths with his handwriting that only he
can decipher.

All powerful-one, why do you not teach us to read your book?
Why do you not move your finger along the letters
and teach us to piece them together and understand like
children?

But no, that you do not do. You are no schoolmaster,
You let things be as they are, incomprehensible as they are.

Then, one day in the evening of time, will you delete them
all again,
let everything become darkness, as it was before you arose
from your thoughts
and wandered off to set them down while on your way
with the burning coal in your hand?

Vad upplevde jag den kvällen,
höstkvällen när jag gick efter ved åt mor?
Jag minns den så väl, ingen kväll minns jag som den.
Det var då jag för första gången såg stjärnorna.

Med vedträna i famnen kom jag att se upp i himlen
och då såg jag dem däruppe, omgivna av sitt gränslösa mörker.
Överallt ovanför mig fanns de i en ödslighet utan gräns.

Jag stod alldeles stilla. Och allting försvann för mig,
allt som funnits förut, allt som varit mitt,
min lilla häst med tre ben, min gummiboll,
min glädje att vakna om morgonen,
solskenet, stenkulorna och den stora kulan av glas,
alla mina leksaker.

När jag kom in till mor igen och lade ifrån mig vedträna
                                        vid köksspisen
märktes säkert ingenting särskilt på mig, säkerligen inte.

Men när jag gick och satte mig på min pall långt borta
                                        från de andra
var jag inte längre något barn.

What did I experience that evening,
that evening in fall when I went to fetch wood for Mother?
I remember it so well, I remember no other evening like it.
It was then that for the first time I saw the stars.

With the billets of wood in my arms I came to look up into
the sky,
and then I saw them there, surrounded by a boundless
darkness.
Everywhere above me they existed in a desolation without
end.

I stood there absolutely still. And everything vanished for me,
everything which had been there before, everything which
had been mine,
my little horse with three legs, my rubber ball,
my joy at waking up in the morning,
the sunshine, the stone marbles and the big glass marble,
all my toys.

When I got back to Mother again and set down the logs by
the kitchen range,
certainly there was no noticeable change in me, certainly not.
But when I went and sat down on my footstool far away
from the others,
I was no longer a child.

Med gamla ögon ser jag mig tillbaka.
Allt är så längesen.
En stenig väg
med trötta oxar som vill hem till kvällen,
ett lass, ett gammalt hjulspår, gårdens gråa gavel
med ljus i ena fönstret.
Maderna kring ån
med dimma över svartnat vatten —

Varför minns jag detta? Vad har jag med det att göra?
Mitt liv förflöt långt borta
i en annan värld. Som i en annan värld.
Och nu är allt snart slut
och gör detsamma.
Var mänskan föds,
var hennes levnad börjar,

With old eyes I look back.
All is so long ago.
A stony road
with weary oxen homesick at eventide,
a wagon, an old cart-track, the farm's grey gable
with a light in one of the windows.
The marshy meadows beside the little river
with mist over darkened water –

Why do I remember this? What have I to do with it?
My life was spent far away
in another world or as if in another world.
And now all is soon over
and does not matter.
Where man is born,
where his life begins,

för att sen sluta inför dödens portar,
vad betyder det?

En stenig väg,
ett lass, ett gammalt hjulspår —

                         *

Min själ är full av kvällens fattigdom
och av den gamla lagårdslyktans sken
när den bärs kring bland båsen
där djuren sover tungt.
Sen bärs den upp mot huset
och skenet flämtar över trädgårdsgången
                              som ej finnes mer
och stegen hörs utav en mänska död för längesen.
Allt är så längesen.

Min själ är full av kvällens fattigdom
och av den gamla lagårdslyktans sken
på trädgårdsgången upp mot deras gråa gård
som inte finnes mer

Min själ? Vad har min själ med det att göra? Med mader kring
                                             en å
en dimmig kväll, en lagårdslyktas sken —

only to end before the gates of death,
what does that matter?

A stony road,
a wagon, an old cart-track —

*

My soul is full of the evening's desolation
and of the light of the old cowhouse-lantern
when it is carried around the stalls
where the cattle are soundly asleep.
Afterwards it is carried up to the house
and its beams flicker over the garden path which is no more,
and the steps are heard of someone long since dead.
All is so long ago.

My soul is full of the evening's desolation
and the beams of the old cowhouse-lantern
on the garden path up to their grey farm
which is no more.

My soul? What has my soul to do with that? With marches
                                        beside a little river,
a misty evening, the beams of a cow-house lantern —

Min själ är utvald till att söka fjärran,
fördolda ting, att vandra under stjärnor.

En stenig väg, ett lass, ett gammalt hjulspår —

*

Med knäppta händer lyssnar de till ord,
till obegripligt stora ord för mänskosjälen,
med knäppta händer vid ett slitet bord
där aftonvarden tagits bort, en gammal bok
lagts fram i stillheten, i överjordisk stillhet.
En stjärna från ett fjärran land står över gårdens tak av torv,
de dödas gård
i senhöstkvällen.
Där kommer någon in med tunga steg
och ställer från sig lagårdslyktan nervid dörren
och träder in i stjärnans sken.
Nu saknas ingen.
Men de är alla döda.

*

De levde också i en stjärnas sken
när deras tunga arbetsdag var slutad.

My soul has been chosen to search far away
for hidden things, to wander under stars.

A stony road, a wagon, an old cart-track —

                          *

With folded hands they listen to words,
incomprehensibly big words for the human soul,
with folded hands at a worn table
where supper has just been cleared and an old book
brought out in silence, heavenly silence.
A star from a far-off land stands over the turf roof of the
                                    farm,
the house of the dead
in the late fall evening.
Someone enters with heavy tread,
setting the cowhouse-lantern down at the door,
enters into the starlight.
Now none are missing
But all are dead.

                    *

They also lived in the light of a lonely star
when their heavy working day was over.

Tillsammans satt de i dess stilla sken,
en enda stjärnas — inte allas, allas.

Tillsammans...
Vid ett slitet bord.
Med stora trötta arbetshänder.

Varför minns jag detta? Vad har jag med det att göra?

Min själ, brinn ensam med din mörka låga! — —

*

En främling är jag, blev till främling född.
En främling ännu i min levnads höst.
Med gamla ögon ser jag mig tillbaka.

Var kommer vi ifrån? Vad är vår själ?
En dimma över svartnat vatten, en lagårdslyktas sken,
en stjärnas?

Med handen över mina gamla ögon,
                        som var ett barns engång —

... de dödas gård
i senhöstkvällen.

Together they sat in its quiet light
the light of a single star — not of all, of all.

Together . . .
At a worn table
with large tired working hands.

Why do I remember this? What have I to do with it?

Burn alone, my soul, with your dark flame! ——

*

A stranger am I, was a stranger born.
A stranger even in the autumn of my life.
With old eyes I look back.

Where do we come from? What is our soul?
A mist over darkened water, the beam of a cowhouse-lantern,
of a star?

With my hand over my old eyes,
                    which were once those of a child —

. . . the house of the dead
in the late autumn evening.

Där kommer någon in med tunga steg
och ställer från sig lagårdslyktan nervid dörren
och träder in i stjärnans sken.
Nu saknas ingen . . .

Varför minns jag detta?

Someone enters with heavy tread
setting the cowhouse-lantern down at the door
enters into the starlight.
Now none are missing . . .

Why do I remember this?

(R)

Som molnen,
som fjärilen,
som den lätta andningen på en spegel —

Tillfällig,
föränderlig,
borta på en liten stund.

O herre över alla himlar, alla världar, alla öden,
vad har du menat med mig?

Like the clouds,
like a butterfly,
like the light breathing on a mirror —

Accidental,
transitory,
gone in a short while.

Lord over all heavens, all worlds, all fates,
what have you meant by me?

En främling är min vän, en som jag inte känner.
En främling långt långt borta.
För hans skull är mitt hjärta fullt av nöd.
För att han inte finns hos mig.
För att han kanske inte alls finns?

Vem är du som uppfyller mitt hjärta med din frånvaro?
Som uppfyller hela världen med din frånvaro?

My friend is a stranger, someone I do not know.
A stranger far, far away.
For his sake my heart is full of disquiet
because he is not with me.
Because, perhaps, after all he does not exist?

Who are you who so fill my heart with your absence?
Who fill the entire world with your absence?

Vad är djupt som saknad.
Vad fyller hjärtat så som tomhet.
Vad uppfyller själen så som längtan efter något som inte finns,
som den vet inte finns.

Andra får ro hos dig.
Andra brinner i din eld, vilar i dina lågande armar.
Men vad är deras lycka
mot min tomhet,
deras glödande förening med dig
mot min ensamhet.

What is as deep as absence?
What fills the heart like emptiness?
What fills the soul like longing for something that does not
                                                    exist,
which it knows does not exist?

Others find peace in you.
Others burn in your fire, rest in your burning arms.
But what is their bliss
compared with my emptiness,
their glowing union with you
compared with my loneliness.

Den gud som inte finns,
det är han som tänder min själ i lågor.
Som gör min själ till en ödemark,
till en rykande mark, en svedjemark som ryker efter eld.
För att han inte finns.
Det är han som frälsar min själ genom att göra den utarmad
och förbränd.
Den gud som inte finns.
Den fruktansvärde guden.

The god who does not exist,
he it is who enkindles my soul,
who makes my soul a wilderness,
a reeking ground, a scorched land, reeking after a fire.
Because he does not exist.
He it is who saves my soul by making it a desert
and scorched.
The god who does not exist.
The awesome god.

Det är inte gud som älskar oss, det är vi som älskar honom.
Som sträcker oss efter honom i längtan efter något annat,
                            något utöver oss själva,
så som kärleken gör.
Och vår längtan blir hetare ju mindre den besvaras,
vår förtvivlan djupare ju mer vi förstår att vi är övergivna.
Att vi är älskade av ingen.

Vad är djupt som saknad, som obesvarad kärlek.

It is not god who loves us, it is we who love him,
who reach out for him in longing after something else,
                                  someone greater than ourselves,
as love does.
And our longing becomes the more intense the less it is
                                  returned,
our despair the deeper the more we realize that we are
                                  deserted,
that we are loved by no one.

What is deeper than absence, than unreturned love?

Om du tror på gud och någon gud inte finns
så är din tro ett ändå större under.
Då är den verkligen någonting ofattbart stort.

Varför ligger det en varelse nere i mörkret och ropar på
något som inte finns?
Varför förhåller det sig så?
Det finns ingen som hör att någon ropar i mörkret. Men varför
finns ropet?

If you believe in god and no god exists
then your belief is an even greater wonder.
Then it is really something inconceivably great.

Why should a being lie down there in the darkness crying to
someone who does not exist?
Why should that be?
There is no one who hears when someone cries in the darkness.
But why does that cry exist?

Spjutet är kastat och vänder aldrig tillbaka.
Glödande skall det genomfara mörkret
i sin heliga båge.

Utslungat är det för alltid
med sin lågande spets
och ännu inte födda mänskohjärtan väntar att genomborras
av det.

Utslungat är spjutet för alltid.

*

Vems är handen som slungade spjutet,
vem är spjutkastaren?

Någon måste ha kastat det
och att döma av kraften bör det ha varit en mäktig hand.

The spear has been cast and will never fly back.
Glowing, its holy arc
will traverse the darkness.

With its glowing point it is cast forth
for ever and ever,
and unborn hearts wait to be pierced by it.

The spear is cast forth for ever and ever.

*

Whose hand hurled the spear?
Who is the spear-caster?

Someone must have cast it
and judging from the power, it must have been a mighty hand.

Vem är han som slungat sin andes spjutspets genom mörkret,
vem är spjutkastaren?

Det är jag, den genomborrade, som frågar.

*

Vänd dig om och försök att upptäcka honom.
Vänd dig om, du som inte träffades framifrån av hans spjut,
du som genomborrades av det under flykten,
flykten undan honom.

Varför talar du om en spjutkastare?
Du trodde ju inte ens på spjutet förrän det träffade dig,
du såg aldrig dess heliga båge i mörkret.
Du trodde inte på det som du flydde ifrån
och spjutspetsen överraskade ditt hjärta som en ljungeld.

Spjutkastaren känner ingen.
Men hans eld känner du.
Varför är det inte nog för dig?
Varför ser du långt bort
när hans spjutspets brinner i ditt hjärta?

Who has hurled his spirit's spear-point through the darkness?
Who is the spear-caster?

It is I, the pierced one, who ask.

*

Turn round and try to find him.
You were not struck by his spear from the front,
you were pierced from behind
while fleeing from him.

Why do you speak of a spear-caster?
You did not even believe in the spear until it hit you,
you never saw its holy arc in the darkness,
you did not believe in what you fled from,
and the spear-point surprised your heart like a stroke of
                                                lightning.

The spear-caster is known to no one.
But you feel his fire.
Why is that not enough for you?
Why do you look away into the distance
when his spear-point burns at your heart?

Öppna ditt hus för mig.
Öppna alla dörrar, alla portar för mig,
som kommer som en stormvind.

När jag drar in i ditt hus skall där inte längre finnas
                              något rum för dig,
du skall bo i öknen som en utstött.
Jag skall driva ut dig i öknen,
du skall ligga naken i öknen under stjärnorna.

Men i det som varit ditt hus skall jag bo,
det skall vara uppfyllt av mig.

Throw open your house to me,
open all doors and gates to me,
as I enter like a storm wind.

When I march in, there will no longer be any room for you,
you shall dwell in the desert as an outcast,
I shall drive you out into the desert,
you shall lie naked in the desert under the stars.

But in the house which has been yours I shall live,
I shall fill it with my presence.

Det är bara det glödande
som blir aska.
Askan är helig.

Du rörde vid mig
och jag blev till aska.
Mitt jag, mitt själv blev till aska, förtärt av dig.

Så säger den älskande och den troende.
Du rörde vid mig. Jag är helig.
Inte jag men min aska är helig.

Only that which smolders
can become ashes.
Ashes are holy.

You touched me
and I became ashes.
My ego, my self turned to ashes, consumed by you.

So say the lover and the believer.
You touched me. I am holy.
That is, not I but my ashes are holy.

Låt min skugga försvinna i din.
Låt mig förlora mig själv
under de stora träden.
De som själva förlorar sin krona i skymningen,
överlämnar sig åt himmelen och natten.

Let my shadow disappear into yours.
Let me lose myself
under the tall trees,
that themselves lose their crowns in the twilight,
surrendering themselves to the sky and the night.

Håll mig i din okända hand
och släpp mig inte.
För mig på morgonljusa broar
över de svindlande djup
där du håller mörkret fängslat.

Men mörkret fängslar man inte länge.
Snart skall det vara afton över dina broar
och natt.
Och kanske skall jag vara mycket ensam.

Hold me in your unknown hand,
and do not let go of me.
Carry me over morning-bright bridges,
and over the dizzy depths
where you keep darkness imprisoned.

But darkness cannot be imprisoned long.
Soon it will be evening over your bridges,
then night.
And perhaps I shall be very lonely.

Att hjärtats oro aldrig må vika.
Att jag aldrig må få frid.
Att jag aldrig må försona mig med livet, inte heller
med döden.
Att min väg må vara oändlig, med ett okänt mål.

May my heart's disquiet never vanish.
May I never be at peace.
May I never be reconciled to life, nor to death either.
May my path be unending, with death its unknowable goal.

V

Från mitt väsens yta blåser han bort den gråa hinnan
och gör mig levande
som en mörk källa.
Lycklig speglar jag hans himmel
och de ljusa molnen kring hans panna.

I min mörka källa
speglar han sitt djup av ljus.

From the surface of my being he blows away the grey film
and makes me alive
like a dark well.
Happily I mirror his sky
and the bright clouds around his forehead.

In my dark well
he mirrors his depth of light.

Det kanske var en dag som alla andra,
men det var då det lyste så i gräset
efter det korta, lätta sommarregnet
och var så långt till aftonen och natten.
En vanlig dag,
men det var då du skulle tackat solen, marken, molnen.

Perhaps it was a day like all the others,
but one with extraordinary gleaming in the grass
after the short, light summer rain,
and it was so far to the evening and the night.
An ordinary day,
but one for giving thanks to the sun, the grass, the clouds.

(R)

SKAPELSEMORGON

I

Fågelunge lyft din vinge,
lyft från min hand
och flyg in i solen, som jag lovar skall komma.
Flyg över den sovande marken
som skall vakna full av blommor
men ännu inte anar någonting.
Flyg genom skymningen
över allt som skall leva.

THE MORNING OF CREATION

I

Fledgling, stretch your wings,
take flight from my hand,
and fly into the sun which I promise shall appear.
Fly over the sleeping earth,
which will wake up full of flowers,
but still divines nothing.
Fly through the twilight
over everything that lives.

Jag är fågelungen som inte är född i något bo.
I en hand, en underlig främmande hand är jag född
och kan inte glömma mitt rede.

Nu finns det många fåglar, men jag är ändå ensam.
Jag flyger bort från de andras skara.
Jag kan inte glömma den hand där jag är född,
den underliga främmande lukten i hans hand,
han som lät mig födas.

II

I am the fledgling that was not born in any nest.
In a hand, a mysterious unknown hand, I was born,
and cannot forget my nest.

Of course, there are many birds, but I remain solitary.
I fly away from the flocks of the others.
I cannot forget the hand where I was born,
the mysterious unknown fragrance of the hand
of him who let me be born.

III

Med smärta vaknar vi blommor till vårt liv på marken.
Smärtsamt lämnar vi den mörka jorden, där allting var
så tryggt.
Det är så tryggt att inte leva.
Smärtsamt öppnar vi oss för den livgivande solen
och varelser som vi inte alls känner går kring bland oss
och talar om vår skönhet.
Men vi förstår ingenting. Vi är blinda som jorden, som vi
har kommit ifrån.
Han ville inte ge oss förmågan att själva se vår härlighet.

Sköna? Inne i oss själva är vi inte sköna.
Det är vi kanske när solen strålar över oss. Men inne i
oss själva råder det ständigt mörker.

III

Grieving, we flowers awake to our life on the earth.
Grieving, we leave the dark earth where everything was so safe.
It is so safe not to live.
Grieving, we open ourselves to the life-giving sun,
and beings of whom we know nothing walk in our midst and
                                   speak of our beauty.
But we understand nothing. We are blind like the earth we
                                   have come from.
He did not want to grant us the power to see ourselves in our
                                   splendor.

Beautiful? Within ourselves we are not beautiful.
Perhaps we are when the sun shines over us. But within
                                   ourselves there is constant darkness.

IV

Jag är en sky, en sky i jordens himmel.
Jag blev till denna underbara morgon och skall strax
                                   utplånas igen.
Jag är så lycklig över att jag bara lever denna morgon,
att jag föds och dör med den
och att det är den strålande solen som skall komma
                                   mig att dö.

IV

I am a cloud, a cloud in the sky above the earth.
I came into being on this wonderful morning and shall soon
                                        be effaced again.
I am so happy because I shall only live this morning,
so happy that I was born and shall die with it,
and that it is the beaming sun which will make me die.

V

Jag är himlen. Jag sluter in allt i min blåa kappa
som jag fått av min älskade.
Han gav mig också ett underbart smycke, ett diadem av
stjärnor kring mitt huvud.
Han måtte älska mig mycket.
Jag älskar också honom.
Men jag har aldrig sett honom.
Man säger att man inte kan se honom.
Och varför skulle man göra det? Inte behöver man se
sin älskade.
Han är hos mig om natten när hans smycke strålar kring
mitt huvud.

V

I am the sky. I enfold all things in my blue cloak,
which I have received from my beloved.
He also gave me wonderful jewels, a diadem of stars
                    to wear around my head.
He must love me very much.
I love him too,
though I have never seen him.
It is said that one cannot see him,
but why should one. One does not have to see
                    one's beloved.
He is with me at night when his diadem glitters
                    around my neck.

VI

Jag är den mörka stjärnan jorden.
I mig gror allt liv, men själv lever jag inte.
Jag är döden som ger liv.
Jag är mörkret som dricker ljus,
som genom sin osläckliga törst efter ljuset ger upphov
                                        till allt liv.
Jag är den mörka stjärnan.
Alla de döda vilar hos mig.

VI

I am the dark star Earth.
In me all things come to life, but I myself do not live.
I am death that gives life.
I am the darkness that drinks the light,
that through its unquenchable thirst for light gives birth
to all life.
I am the dark star.
All the dead rest with me.

VII

I mig blåste han in sin ande.
Därför är allting så svårt för mig.
Stjärnorna vandrar över min himmel och ger mig
ingen ro.
Och genom min själ vältrar dunkla skapelsetöcken.
Min dag är full av ljus, min natt är utan gräns.
Jag är människan. Mig hände det fruktansvärda
att han blåste in sin egen själ i mig.

VII

Into me he breathed his spirit.
That is why everything is so difficult for me.
The stars wander over my sky and give me no peace,
and the dark clouds of creation whirl through my soul.
My day is full of light, my night is without limits.
I am Man. To me the dreadful thing happened, namely,
that he breathed his own soul into me.

VIII

Jag är stjärnan som speglar sig i dig.
Din själ skall vara stilla,
annars kan jag inte spegla mig i den.
Din själ är mitt hem. Jag har inget annat.

Men hur skulle du kunna vara stilla när mitt ljus
skälver i din själ.

VIII

I am the star that mirrors itself in you.
Your soul shall be serene and calm,
otherwise I cannot mirror myself in it.
Your soul is my home. I have no other.

But how could you be serene when my light
                                    quivers in your soul.

Jag är handen som fågelungen lämnade,
skaparens hand.
Aldrig vänder den tillbaka till mig,
till sitt rede.
Ingenting vänder tillbaka till mig.

Var är skyarna, blommorna och vindarna,
var är fågelungen som låg så mjuk och varm hos mig?
Var är mitt verk som fyllde mig med värme och lycka?
En morgon, en morgon för längesen.

Jag är redet som längtar efter sin fågelunge.
Jag är skaparens tomma hand.

IX

I am the hand from which the fledgling flew,
the hand of the creator.
It will never return to me,
to its nest.
Nothing returns to me.

Where are the clouds, the flowers and the winds?
Where is the fledgling that lay so soft and warm with me?
Where is my work which filled me with warmth and happiness?
One morning, one morning, long ago.

I am the nest which longs for its fledgling.
I am the creator's empty hand.

I den stilla aftonfloden
såg jag det ställe där han speglade sitt ansikte engång
i avskedsstunden, innan han färdades vidare.
Vinden visade det för mig,
den sorgsna vinden som på hans befallning strök bort hans
                              bild från vattnet
och som ännu sörjer över att den måste göra det.

Svårmodigt berättade den för mig om honom,
om hans ansikte, som den hade rört vid,
och om hans bild i aftonfloden
innan det skymde och mörkret kom
som nu.

På en flotte av säv färdades han över.

Varför sitter jag här ännu vid stranden som han lämnat
                              för så längesen?

In the silent river of evening
I saw the place where once, only once, his face was reflected,
at the hour of departure before he continued his journey.
The wind showed it to me,
the sorrowing wind which at his command erased his
                                        image from the waters,
and still grieves because it had to obey.

Heavy at heart, it told me of him,
of his face which it had touched,
and his image in the river of evening,
before nightfall and darkness came,
as they now have.

On a raft of rushes he crossed the river.

Why do I still sit here on the shore which he left
                        so long ago?

appendix

[Note: The prose versions of poems not translated by Mr. Auden have been included in this book at the explicit request of the publisher, to make the parallel text complete. They appear with my great reservations. My "transliterations," as I prefer to call them, are offered without suggestions of alternative choices of phrasing and with no discussion of the choices made. Six of the eleven poems were heavily rhymed, inferior, or otherwise unsuited for translation, in Mr. Auden's opinion. L.S.]

Allt är så underligt fjärran idag,
så långt långt borta.
Inne i molnen hörs vingarnas slag
av fåglar, långt långt borta.

Klar som en klocka av silver och glas,
långt långt borta,
ljuder en fågelröst spröd som glas
i en himmel långt långt borta.

Ensam i kvällsljuset lyssnar jag.
Vad dagarna börjar bli korta.
Hösten har kommit. Snart skymmer min dag.
Jag hör vingar så långt långt borta.

Everything is so strangely removed today,
so far far away.
Within the clouds is heard the beating of the wings
of birds, far far away.

Clear as a bell of silver and glass,
far far away,
a bird's voice resounds brittle as glass
in a sky far far away.

Alone in the light of evening I hearken.
How the days begin to shorten.
Autumn has come. Soon my day will grow dim.
I hear wings so far far away.

Du sträcker ut din skymningshand
och plågad själ får vila,
du släcker hjärtats tunga brand
och leder genom aftonland
den trötte till hans vila.

I nattlig jord du sänker ner
det liv som tycks förhärjat,
som såningsmannen återger
åt jorden som han öppen ser
den skörd som han har bärgat.

You stretch out your twilight-hand
and tormented soul gets rest,
you quench the heart's heavy flame
and lead through evening land
the tired one to his rest.

Into nocturnal ground you lower
the life which seems laid waste,
like the sower returning
to the earth which he sees open
the harvest that he has gathered.

Hjorten ser förundrad ner på jägarn
som är död på mossan ini skogen,
sänker huvudet med tunga kronan
över blod som sipprar fram ur bröstet.

Kan ett väsen såsom detta blöda?
Kan det onda dö som vi i skogen?
Ligga så, med alltför stora ögon
och med blicken fylld av hjälplös fråga?

Vad är då dess makt, när själv det segnar
ner som vi, de vapenlösa,
och är fyllt av samma stumma ångest,
samma gåta i den brustna blicken?

Wonderstruck the deer looks down at the hunter
who is dead on the moss in the forest,
lowers his head with its heavy crown
over the blood that oozes from his chest.

Can such a being bleed?
Can evil die like us in the forest?
Lie like this, with too large eyes
and with a gaze filled with helpless question?

What then is its power, if itself it drops
down like us, the unarmed,
and is filled by the same mute anguish,
the same enigma in the broken gaze?

GAMMAL GENIUS

Tunga är vingarna,
tyngre än jag,
kan mig ej längre lyfta.
Någonstans ovanför
är det väl dag,
men inte här i min klyfta.

Något inom mig
var större än jag,
kom mig att högre syfta.
Tung är min vinge,
tunga dess slag,
kan mig ej längre lyfta.

OLD GENIUS

Heavy are the wings,
heavier than I,
can no longer lift me.
Somewhere above
there is surely day,
but not here in my abyss.

Something inside me
was greater than I,
made me aim higher.
Heavy is my wing,
heavy its strokes,
can no longer lift me.

Engång mot himlen
steg jag i ljus,
upp mot det oerhörda.
Jublande hörde jag
vingarnas brus,
dem jag nu bär som en börda.

Skönt är att leva,
skönt är att tro,
skönt är det oerhörda.
Tungt är att gammal
i klyftorna bo
och bära sin själ som en börda.

Once towards heaven
I rose in light,
up towards the ineffable.
Jubilant I heard
the soughing of wings,
those which now I carry like a burden.

Glorious it is to live,
glorious it is to believe,
glorious is the ineffable.
Heavy it is to live,
old, in the abysses
and to carry one's soul like a burden.

Gissa din gåta, lillebror,
som jag vaggar i kväll under stjärnor.
Himlarna mörknar och världen är stor,
vaggan är upphängd i stjärnor.

Gissa din gåta, din och min,
och sen kan du somna så stilla
i dina vackraste drömmar in
och intet skall göra dig illa.

Guess your riddle, baby brother,
whom I rock to sleep tonight beneath stars.
The skies darken and the world is vast,
the cradle is suspended in stars.

Guess your riddle, yours and mine,
and then you can fall asleep so quietly
in your most beautiful dreams
and nothing will do you harm.

Säg mig du eviga stjärna,
varför stirrar du ner i mig.
Som fienden spejar ur fjärran
så vaktar du ständigt på mig.

Vass är din blick och den borrar
sig ner, djupt ner i min själ.
Spjutspets ur evigheten,
du vill mig nog inte väl.

Jag är ej evig, mitt väsen
rinner i sanden ut.
Varför då genomborra
mig med ditt lågande spjut?

Tell me you eternal star
why do you stare down at me.
Like the enemy spying from afar
so you can constantly watch me.

Sharp is your gaze and it pierces down
deep down in my soul.
Spear-point from eternity,
you surely do not desire my good.

I am not eternal, my being
runs out into the sand.
Why then pierce me through
with your flaming spear?

Det mesta är så betydelselöst.
Men så finns det någonting oerhört som stiger upp som
                    ett glödande moln på himlen
och förtär allt.
Då blir allting förvandlat
och du själv förvandlad
och det som nyss tycktes dig av största värde
har inget värde alls för dig mer.
Och du går bort genom alltings aska
och är själv aska.

Det mesta är så betydelselöst.

Most things are so unimportant.
But then there is something ineffable which ascends like
                    a glowing cloud in the sky
and consumes everything.
Then everything becomes transformed
and you yourself [become] transformed
and what moments ago seemed to you of the greatest value
has no value at all to you.
And you walk away through the ashes of everything
and are yourself ashes.

Most things are so unimportant.

MORGONEN

Älskliga varelse, morgon med rosenläppar,
sjung för mig.
Sjung en sång, tidig och klar som dagg, som ungt glas,
en sång som förvandlar allt.

THE MORNING

Delightful being, morning with rosy lips,
sing for me.
Sing a song, early and clear like dew, like young glass,
a song that transfigures everything.

Morgonriket med sin himmel av honung
ligger och väntar med slutna ögon,
med alla blommornas slutna ögon.
Vacker som en kvinna, som tusen kvinnor,
ligger hon och blundar med blommande ögon,
ligger och väntar under sin honungshimmel
på sin konung, den hänsynslösa dagen.

The morning land with its sky of honey
lies and waits with closed eyes,
with all the flowers' closed eyes.
Beautiful like a woman, like a thousand women,
she lies with shut and flowery eyes,
lies waiting beneath its honey sky
for its king, the inconsiderate day.

Nu är det sommarmorgon
och jordens högtidsstund,
nu ringer blåa klockor
sin frid i helig lund
av rönnar, björk och sälg.
Nu är det jordisk helg.

Nu sänker himlen stilla
sig över jorden ner
och lyss till hennes klockor
som den i grönskan ser.
I andakt allting står
som spröda klangen når.

Långt bort är kalla stjärnor,
långt bort är gränslös rymd,
men av det sommarblåa
all sorg är undanskymd.
Allt är blott jordisk frid
en stund vid sommartid.

Now it is summer-morning
and the earth's season of joy,
now the blue bells ring
their peace in holy grove
of rowan, birch, and sallow.
Now it is earthly hallow day.

Now the sky serenely lowers
itself onto the earth
and listens to her bells
which it sees in the verdure.
Everything to which the soft chime reaches
stands in devotion.

Far away are cold stars,
far away is boundless space,
but from the summer blue
all sorrow is concealed.
Everything is just earthly peace
for a while in summer time.

Tacka vill jag blommorna och molnen,
träden och sommarhimmeln,
det svala morgonljuset
och kvällsvinden som stryker över ljungen.
Så som den som bryter upp ifrån ett gästfritt hus
där ingenting fattas, där han bjudits på allt,
så vill jag tacka för hemmet jag gästat, för människohemmet.
Med handen på grinden vill jag se mig tillbaka, som om jag
skulle kunna minnas det som jag lämnar.
Och sedan vill jag se framåt igen, fastän hemlös.

I wish to thank the flowers and the clouds,
the trees and the summer sky,
the cool morning light
and the evening wind that sweeps past the heather.
Like the one who breaks up from a hospitable house
where nothing is lacking,
               where everything has been put on the table
I then want to [express my] thank[s] for the home in which
              l stayed as a guest, for the human home.
With my hand on the gate I wish to look back, as if
              I could remember what I will leave.
And then I want to look forward again, although homeless.

Pär Lagerkvist (1891–1974), Swedish novelist and poet, published *Evening Land* (original title *Aftonland*) in 1953. In it he contemplates approaching old age, the mystery of life and of God, and the proximity of death.

W. H. Auden and Leif Sjöberg, the translators, have previously collaborated in translating the poems of Swedish poets Gunnar Ekelöf and Werner Aspenström. Their best-known co-translation is probably that of *Markings* by Dag Hammarskjöld (1964).

The book was designed by Julie Paul. The typeface for the text is Aldine roman designed by IBM; and the display face is Albertus designed by Berthold Wolpe in the 1930s.

The text is printed by Nashoba text paper and the book is bound in Holliston Mills' Roxite vellum finish cloth over binders boards.

Manufactured in the United States of America.